A FACE IN THE WINDOW

A J Witt.

Paperback
ISBN: 978-1-916954-40-3

Table of Contents

Dedication

To my granddaughters, who always loved to listen to my stories and always provided enough mischief to keep me inspired and to Sheba, the best dog ever.

Chapter I
The Phone Call

"Mom, it's Aunt Risi," Emily yelled. "Your weird aunt," she whispered, giving Mom the phone.

"Be quiet, she'll hear you," Mom whispered.

Mom said hello and then listened and nodded as Aunt Risi did all of the talking.

"Okay," Mom finally said after what seemed like a really long time.

"We'll be happy to take care of it. Talk to you tomorrow evening."

Emily could hardly stand still. "What's going on, what does she want, is she coming here?" she asked as she followed Mom back to the kitchen with Sheba, her black lab, close behind.

"I didn't think you'd be interested since Aunt Risi is so weird," Mom said with a grin on her pretty face.

"Come on, tell me," Emily squealed. She was ready to burst and wouldn't sleep all night if she didn't find out what the phone call was all about.

"Okay, okay, I wouldn't want you to explode," Mom said, laughing. "It seems Aunt Risi has bought a house, which she has never seen except for some pictures, somewhere near here."

"No way," Emily said. "She can't move here. It's bad enough when she comes for a visit."

"She's a good person, and she loves us. You could learn a lot from her," Mom said.

"She's just too weird. She's lived in too many weird places," Emily said.

"She's eccentric, Emily; there's a difference. Anyway, there's more, the house is very old and filled with antiques. No one has lived there for fifty years. With the help of the realtor Aunt Risi has arranged for the water, phone and electricity to be turned on tomorrow morning, but she can't be here until next week. She wants us to pick up the keys from the realtor and be on hand to supervise when the utility people arrive. We'll leave first thing in the morning."

"Oh great, just what I want to do on my first day of summer vacation."

Mom had a strange look on her face.

"There's more, isn't there?" Emily said.

"She wants you and Sheba to stay with her when she arrives. She wants to get to know you better; besides, she'll need some help."

Emily's big blue eyes got even bigger. "No way," she choked out when she found her voice. "I am not going to spend my entire summer vacation with weird Aunt Risi."

"It's not your entire summer vacation, it will only be two weeks, and I will stop over every few days. She's invited Zachary too."

"That's even worse. I hope the two of them have a great time together."

"Just think about it," Mom said. "We'll pick up the keys first thing in the morning and don't leave your usual trail of personal belongings on your way up the stairs."

Emily just rolled her eyes at Mom and headed for the stairs. As she got ready for bed, she remembered the last time she saw her cousin and once best friend Zachary and the fight they had.

"You are always so bossy," Zachary had said. "Just because you are twelve you think you know everything."

"When you have a detective agency someone has to be in charge and it certainly can't be you, you're only eleven. You don't know anything." Emily remembered saying.

"That's it," Zachary had said. "I'm leaving and I'm not coming back. You can't boss me around anymore."

That was a year ago. Then, Zachary and his family moved away.

He never even called to say goodbye.

Chapter II
Calibeary Lane

"Emily, hurry up, it's time to go," Mom called up the stairs.

Emily was trying to hurry, but she couldn't do anything with her unruly blond hair and couldn't find one of her shoes. She raced down the stairs with Sheba at her heels.

"Help me find my shoe." She said to Sheba as she squeezed her slender body between the sofa and the bookcase. Sheba found the missing shoe behind the chair and dropped it on the floor while Emily squeezed herself back out.

"Good girl, Sheba," she said as she ran to the bathroom to give her hair another try. She gave up, grabbed her baseball cap, and ran to the kitchen where Mom was waiting, keys in hand.

"One day I'm just going to leave without you," Mom said as she started the car.

It was a short trip to the realtor's office. Emily and Sheba waited in the car while Mom got the keys and some directions.

"It's a little further away than Aunt Risi thought," Mom said when she returned to the car. "But the directions are easy, so we should find it okay."

"Have you thought about Aunt Risi's invitation?"

"I can't stay with her, Mom she's just too weird," Emily said. "I can see it now; she'll get off the plane wearing something from every country she's ever been in. She'll have a ton of makeup on, some huge earrings, and let's not forget, the goofy hat. Everyone will stare. What if she wants to go out in public, or even worse, what if she wants to go to one of those weird shops in that creepy alley like last time? What if my friends see me? Zachary is weird, too. Why would I want to spend time with him?"

"You can't expect everyone to be the way you think they should be," Mom said as they turned onto Calibeary Lane. "Aunt Risi is different and there is nothing wrong with that. Maybe Zachary thinks you're weird. What if he doesn't want to spend time with you?"

Emily's reply stuck in her throat. They both stared silently at the mansion looming before them. It was huge, three stories tall, four counting the tower. A gray stone structure with a red tile roof. All the windows appeared to be shuttered except for the tower. A front porch with huge pillars provided a balcony off one of the second-floor bedrooms. An outside stairway led from the second floor to the third floor. The grounds were overgrown and surrounded by a tall black iron fence with stone pillars at the drive. It was very grand and must have been quite majestic in its day.

Maybe staying with Aunt Risi wouldn't be such a bad idea, after all, Emily thought as numerous possibilities popped into her head.

The front entrance led them into a large, dark hall. To the right of the door, a curved open stairway gracefully led the way to the second floor. On the left, the parlor beckoned.

Emily and Mom were speechless. Even Sheba stood motionless.

It was as though they had stepped back in time. Except for some dust and a few spiderwebs, the furnishings were in perfect order, right down to the open book on the parlor table.

"Wow," Emily whispered, pulling Sheba closer. "This place has to be hiding a mystery, or at least a ghost story or two."

The stairs provided a beautifully carved, arched entrance to the dining room, and swinging doors led the way to the kitchen.

Emily wanted to continue the tour, but the utility people arrived, so Mom went to make sure they followed Aunt Risi's instructions. Emily and Sheba found themselves back in the main hall, but only for a short time. Beyond the Parlor, Emily spied an open door and couldn't resist a little peak.

"Wow," Emily said. "This is unreal; like something you would see in a movie." It was gloomy and dark, and Emily felt cold as she entered the library.

Sheba stayed close to Emily as they walked around the room. Emily examined some books and soon found herself happily seated at the huge, old desk, reading articles and letters about a wealthy family named Calibeary and how they built Calibeary Manor on Calibeary Lane.

It seemed like no time had passed when Mom came in to say it was time to go.

On the steps, Emily suddenly felt they were being watched. Chills ran up her spine. She looked all around but didn't see anything. Walking toward the car, the feeling was even stronger. She could feel the hair on the back of her neck stand as her eyes scanned the wooded grounds.

As they drove away, Emily looked back at Calibeary Manor.

For a split second, she thought she saw something in the tower window. Probably just the sun's reflection, Emily thought.

She looked again. No, something had definitely moved. A face.

There was a face in the tower window. "Mom, stop," Emily cried.

"What's the matter?"

Emily changed her mind. She couldn't tell Mom about the face. Then Mom might say she couldn't go in the tower. And that was what Emily decided to do. I'll get to the bottom of this, she thought.

"I think I'll stay with Aunt Risi after all," Emily told Mom.

"That would be great," Mom said, used to Emily's outbursts. "Aunt Risi will be so pleased."

Chapter III
Aunt Risi Has Landed

Emily touched Mom's arm as she spotted the huge, weird hat approaching the airport gate. It was part Southern Plantation and part African Safari, with strange-looking signs and pins all over it.

"Told you," Emily said. "I can't wait to see the rest of her."

Mom just laughed as they waited for the other passengers to move on.

"It's even worse than I imagined," Emily said when they finally got the full view. Below the huge hat, Aunt Risi wore cannonball earrings from who knows where. Her clothes were a combination of Australian Out Back and Austrian Beer Garden with tall brown boots. Her bag was a charming old world tapestry, but as usual, it didn't match her outfit. She had a look of joy on her face, and her blue eyes sparkled with mischief.

They stepped forward to hug Aunt Risi, and they all started talking at once.

"How are you," Mom said.

"It's good to see you," Emily said

"My how you've grown," Aunt Risi said.

Mom and Aunt Risi continued to talk as they walked to the baggage claim. They waited for what seemed like forever for the luggage to come down. Finally, they had all Aunt Risi's luggage and headed for the car.

"Where is that beautiful dog of yours?" Aunt Rise asked as they loaded her luggage in the car.

"She's at home," Mom said. "We didn't know how long we would be, and we didn't want to leave her in the car too long. We'll pick her up along with Emily's things on the way."

Sheba was waiting by the front door along with Emily's suitcase, which Mom had helped her pack the night before. Piled in the back seat with Sheba, Emily started having second thoughts about staying with Aunt Risi, but as the mansion came into view, she knew she had to see this through. She had to find out who belonged to the face in the window and why they were in Aunt Risi's house.

If Aunt Risi was surprised as they drove up, she didn't show it; she acted like it was quite what she expected. Sheba sniffed and shied away from the door as they walked up the front steps. She didn't want to go in. Emily had to lead her inside.

"No one has been here but Dad and I when we dropped the groceries off last night," Mom said as she went ahead to open the door.

Once inside, Sheba seemed to relax a little, so they took the luggage upstairs, and Emily got her first look at the second floor.

An open sitting room decorated in lace and giant spider webs greeted them at the top of the stairs. The huge master bedroom was next. The oversized room took up almost half of the front side of the second floor.

"This is wonderful," Aunt Risi said. "I love this house already.

"I hope everything works in the adjoining bathroom."

The last room on the front side of the hall was where Emily chose to sleep. "The spider webs are the size of Texas," Emily said once she overcame the shock. "I sure hope the spiders have moved on."

"Zachary will be here in two days," Aunt Risi said. "Let's see which room will be okay for him."

"He'll be thrilled," Mom said when they saw another bedroom decorated with the same huge spider webs.

"Wonder what's on the third floor?" Emily asked.

"The realtor said it was the servant's quarters. Four bedrooms, a large sitting room, a kitchen and two bathrooms," Aunt Risi said.

"Wow Aunt Risi, are you going to have servants?" Emily asked.

"Well, it is a big house, and I am sure I will need some help to care for it, even with Mimi coming, but it will be fun to explore it all for now. With your help, I think it will be quite an adventure."

"Do you know about the family that used to live here?" Emily asked as they walked downstairs.

"Only a little," Aunt Risi said. "But what I do know has piqued my interest. I can't wait to find out more. I am hoping there will be lots of family history here. Maybe even enough to write a book."

"The day Mom and Sheba and I came for the utilities to be turned on I did a little exploring in the library. I found a bunch of stuff, articles and books piled on the desk," Emily said.

"Did you explore any other rooms?" Aunt Risi asked.

"No," Emily said. "There is so much to see in there. I didn't get any further than the desk. I spent the whole time reading the newspaper articles.

Mom was busy setting out the lunch she had planned for Aunt

Risi's welcome home. "That's strange," Mom said with her head in the refrigerator. "I distinctly remember putting the packages of cold cuts next to this platter I prepared yesterday when Troy and I were here. But I can't find them anywhere."

Emily and Aunt Risi each had a look in the refrigerator. "They are definitely missing," Aunt Risi said.

"Maybe you put it all on the platter after all," Emily said.

"Maybe," Mom said, looking doubtful. "I must have, where else could they have gone."

The face in the window, Emily thought, that's where they went.

After lunch, when Mom went home, Aunt Risi and Emily decided to explore the parlor. Most of the furnishings were antiques, and Aunt Risi was very excited about each piece. As they explored, Sheba stayed very close to Emily. She was a bit nervous in their strange new surroundings.

Emily decided not to tell Aunt Risi about the face in the window, at least not yet. It would be challenging, but she and Sheba had to find a way to get to the tower without Aunt Risi knowing. Zachary would be here in two days. It might be easier to get away from Aunt Risi, then. Maybe he could be of some use after all.

Chapter IV
Strange Happenings

The first night in the mansion was uneventful. Emily climbed out of her sleeping bag and dressed quickly. She raced down the stairs, but Sheba beat her to the kitchen. Aunt Risi was already there drinking tea.

She was dressed in a blue Japanese kimono. Very strange but also kind of pretty, Emily thought as she tried not to laugh.

"Good morning," Aunt Risi said. "Let's get you some breakfast, and then I think we'll start exploring the library. You can show me what you found the first day you were here."

The library was dark and gloomy. It took both Emily and Aunt Risi to pull the heavy window tapestries away so they could open the shutters. With that accomplished, the library was much brighter but far from cheerful. The ceiling was at least 12 feet tall. The shelves went from the floor to the ceiling. A ladder hung from a track that was attached to the ceiling. The track ran all around the room. Emily found herself staring at the desk.

Everything had been moved around, and some books had been added. She shivered from the chill in the air.

"Has anyone else been here?" Emily asked.

"Not that I'm aware of. The realtor gave your mom the keys, and you and your family are the only ones who could get in. Why do you ask?"

"Just wondered," Emily said as she picked up a newspaper article.

"Wow, listen to this. CALIBEARY DAUGHTER BANNED FROM THE MANSION."

"Gabriella Louise Calibeary eloped with Stephen Hadley after quarreling with her father. Joseph Calibeary announced that until she comes to her senses, she is no longer welcome at Calibeary Manor."

"Very interesting," Aunt Risi said. "It makes me wonder if there is some family out there somewhere. Let's collect all that we find in a folder, and then maybe we can put a scrapbook together for the family that might be out there. We can go to one of those lovely little shops on Pigtail Alley to get a scrapbook. Maybe my car will be here by then."

Emily looked at Sheba and rolled her eyes. Another prediction coming true, she thought, but even worse than she imagined, riding in Aunt Risi's old roadster. I wonder what weird outfit she'll wear that day.

They worked quietly until Emily suggested it was time for lunch.

"Let's have sodas," Emily said as she ran into the kitchen and opened the antique refrigerator. "Did you already get them out?"

"No. Something very strange is going on," 'Aunt Risi said from the pantry. "Did you move the snacks?"

"No," Emily said as she joined Aunt Risi in the pantry. The face in the window strikes again, Emily thought. I need to get to the bottom of this and soon.

"If this continues, we'll have to call your mother to bring more supplies."

After a lunch of grilled cheese and tomato soup, they returned to the library. They both immediately noticed the article that was sitting on top of the desk. It was the same article that they had put in the scrapbook folder earlier that morning. Everything else was exactly as they left it.

"Something very strange is going on," Aunt Risi said as she looked up toward the ceiling.

They worked all afternoon and evening, stopping only long enough for a quick supper. Eventually, even Aunt Risi got tired and suggested they turn in.

As Emily crawled into her sleeping bag, Sheba sniffed around the room. She seemed satisfied that everything was okay and hopped up on the bed with Emily. The excitement of the day had worn them both out, and they were soon sound asleep.

The house was silent, and the moonlight in the windows gave the room an eerie glow.

Suddenly, Emily's eyes were wide open, staring at something white near the doorway. At the same moment, Sheba saw it. She started growling and lunged toward the door. It was there and then gone in an instant. Sheba ran into the hall, barking.

"Are you alright dear?" Aunt Risi asked as she ran into the room.

Emily, unable to move, was still staring at the doorway. Suddenly, she flew out of bed and ran into the hall where Sheba stood barking.

"What's going on?" Aunt Risi demanded.

"I don't know, I must have had a nightmare." But as she patted Sheba, Emily knew it wasn't a dream.

"Would you like to tell me about it?" Aunt Risi asked, looking concerned. "Maybe a cup of tea would help."

Emily found herself halfway down the stairs before she could object.

In the large kitchen, Aunt Risi lit a burner on the antique range while Emily found some tea bags and cups. Sheba was uneasy and paced from the table to the doorway, making Emily very nervous.

"Tell me what happened," Aunt Risi said as she poured the tea and sat at the table.

"I don't really know. Maybe reading all those old articles gave me the creeps. I don't remember. I must have yelled in my sleep, and then Sheba started barking.

"But you went charging into the hall as if you were chasing someone."

"I know, I guess I just wasn't quite awake yet. I don't know what I was doing."

"You probably need to rest," Aunt Risi said as she put the tea things away. "You know what can happen on the last night before the dark of the moon. Crawl into bed from the foot and tomorrow night we'll have some lemon balm tea before bed."

Aunt Risi gave Emily a comforting hug, but instead of the concerned expression Emily expected, Aunt Risi actually looked happy. Definitely weird, Emily thought.

After crawling back into bed from the foot, as Aunt Risi told her to, she snuggled in her sleeping bag with Sheba as close as she could get; Emily felt guilty. If she had told Aunt Risi what she thought she saw, she probably would have called the police, and the clues to any mystery would have been ruined. On the other hand, if she had told her she thought she saw a ghost, Aunt Risi might have liked that and called a séance. Either way, there really isn't anything to tell, at least not yet.

Sheba licked Emily's face, and she fell into a very restless sleep.

Aunt Risi, dressed in knickers, was already in the kitchen when Emily and Sheba came down.

"How did you sleep dear?" she asked as Emily poured herself a bowl of cereal.

"Okay," Emily said, not looking Aunt Risi in the eye.

"It was a rather short night, but I hope you're up to continuing our exploration of the library. I am sure we will need to spend at the very least a few more days in there."

While Aunt Risi finished her tea, Emily and Sheba went to the library.

Sheba's hair stood up on her back, and she growled softly. Emily looked around the room and found the same article on the desk again.

"There really are some strange happenings in this place," she said, placing the article back in the folder.

Chapter V
In The Nick of Time

A phone call for Aunt Risi gave Emily and Sheba a break. They raced out of the library, down the hall, and out of the back door. They didn't stop until they were safely hidden, sitting on the bench behind the overgrown rose arbor near the back gate.

"Well, Sheba, it's definitely been a weird day and a half with Aunt Risi, but not as bad as I thought it was going to be. I wonder what can happen the night before the dark of the moon. I have never heard that before. I do wonder about all the dust and spiderwebs. Mom would have had me clean everything before we could explore, but not Aunt Risi."

Sheba barked in agreement.

"She also can keep working nonstop. We need to take more breaks."

Sheba tipped her head to the side and licked Emily's face to comfort her.

"I want to explore the rest of the house, not spend forever in the library. How will we ever find the way to the tower if we never get out of the library, or off the first floor."

Sheba alerted, and Emily jumped off the bench and found herself staring face-to-face with her cousin Zachary.

"Well, well, if it isn't Miss Em and the Queen of Sheba." Sheba was happy to see him even if Emily wasn't.

He was at least a head taller than when Emily had last seen him, and instead of his usual buzz cut, his hair was a little longer and combed to the side. He had slimmed down and was dressed in jeans and a baseball shirt.

After the official greeting between Sheba and Zachary, Emily asked, "How did you find us?"

"Just like old times," Zachary said. "Don't even say hi first, just start asking questions."

"Not when you sneak up on me like that."

"I didn't sneak; I just followed the complaining. If you hadn't been rambling on, you would have heard me call you from the back door."

Emily just glared at him.

"Okay, maybe I did sneak just a little and maybe I deserve whatever you're thinking."

"I'm thinking that you never even called to say goodbye. What do you expect, you think you can just walk back in, and everything will be just as it was before you moved away?"

"Before I moved away, we had a fight. Remember? Let's just start over. Let's call a truce, or at least pretend to get along while we are staying with Aunt Risi," Zachary said.

Emily quickly thought it over. She was kind of happy to see him; maybe she should give him another chance; they would only be there for two weeks after all. Besides, she did need someone to run interference with Aunt Risi while she searched for the stairway or ladder that led to the tower, and there certainly wasn't anyone else around. "Okay, let's give it a try," she said.

"How did you get here? You're early."

"My dad's meeting was changed so he dropped me off at your house late last night and your dad brought me here this morning. Did I hear you say something about the tower?"

Emily looked at Zachary as though she didn't know what he was talking about. She thought I am not sure I want to share this with him right now, but I can't expect him to help me if I don't tell him.

"Okay," she said. "There are some very strange things going on around here, but if I tell you, you have to give me your word, that you won't tell Aunt Risi, at least not yet."

"I should have known you'd be up to something. Okay, you have my word. What's going on?"

"I saw a face in the tower window and strange things have been happening ever since."

"What kind of strange things?"

"Food disappearing, papers and articles moved, books appearing and there was someone in my room last night," Emily said.

Zachary looked a little puzzled.

"Let's sit down, and I'll start at the beginning," Emily said. "The day Mom and I came to let the utility people in, Sheba and I hung out in the library. I found some information about the family that used to live here. Too soon, it was time to go home, so I left everything on the desk. As we drove away, I turned for one last look and saw a face in the tower window. The day before Aunt Risi arrived, Mom and Dad brought some groceries here. Mom fixed a cold cut platter and put the extra packages of cold cuts and cheese in the fridge next to the platter. When we got here from the airport, the extra packages of meat and cheese were missing. Mom said she must have used them, but I don't think so."

"Yesterday morning, I wanted to show Aunt Risi what I had found in the library; all the papers and articles had been moved around, and some books were on the desk. Yesterday, we noticed some sodas and snacks were missing, and someone was in my room last night. I only got a glimpse of something white. Sheba went ballistic; she's been on guard since we arrived. Aunt Risi came flying in to see what was happening, so I told her I had a bad dream."

"Wow," Zach said. "Do you think it was a ghost?"

Emily scowled, "Ghosts don't eat Zachary."

"Oh yeah," Zachary replied, looking a little foolish. "So, what do you think?"

"I don't know. We just have to get to the tower I know we'll find something there."

"This sounds pretty scary. Are you sure we shouldn't tell Aunt Risi?"

Emily glared at Zachary. "If you don't want to help then butt out?"

"Okay, we'll do it your way. Where do we start?"

"We'll think of an excuse to go up to the third floor after lunch. Let's go tell Aunt Risi it's time to eat. She never looks at the clock."

To Emily's surprise, Aunt Risi was already in the kitchen. The pantry door was open, and she was searching through all the shelves.

"The crackers and cheese spread are missing. I have looked everywhere. I hope we can keep better track of things when Mimi gets here," Aunt Risi said.

Emily and Zachary exchanged glances.

"When will that be?" Emily asked, hoping it would be soon. What better reason to explore the third floor than the arrival of Aunt Risi's ancient housekeeper.

"She'll be here this evening," Aunt Risi said. "After lunch we'll explore the third floor."

Chapter VI
A Hidden Portal

The stairway to the third floor was steep and narrow. It was very stuffy, and they were all hot and sticky by the time they got to the top.

Sheba led the way, followed closely by Emily and Zachary. Aunt Risi, moving a little slower, brought up the rear. They soon found themselves standing in a huge, open sitting room. It was fully furnished, although less elegantly than the first and second floors. The dust was twice as thick and loaded with spider webs. Emily saw a few spiders and carefully skirted around them as she walked to the center of the big room. There were two matching brown leather sofas, two overstuffed chairs, and a wooden rocker. A dining table and chairs stood at the far end, and a small kitchen was built into the corner. They opened the shutters, but the windows had years of dust on them, so it was still dark and gloomy. The big room was in the center of the third floor, with two bedrooms on either end.

Emily stood in the middle of the big room, looking around. While Aunt Risi took her time looking over each bedroom, Emily and Zachary raced ahead, looking for a door leading the way to the tower.

"No doors," Emily said as they stood in the last bedroom. "There has to be a door somewhere."

"Let's look again, but a little slower this time," Zach said.

They went back through, avoiding Aunt Risi. They carefully examined each room.

"Nothing," Zachary said.

"Maybe we're not looking for the right thing; maybe there is no door."

"Maybe, just maybe, we should be looking for a secret passage or a secret wall. Let's look again, but this time, go over each wall. Look for anything uneven; look inside each closet. We must find something," Emily said.

Before they finished the third bedroom, Aunt Risi came in. "Mimi will have to decide if she wants to sleep up here. It is pretty secluded, and the stairs are awfully steep."

Emily agreed, and since they didn't find a way to the tower, she hoped Mimi would choose to sleep downstairs because somehow, they would have to get back up to the third floor. It would be easier if no one was staying up there.

"Let's go back to the library. If we finish up in there, we can move to another room tomorrow," Aunt Risi said.

Emily just rolled her eyes at Zachary and followed Aunt Risi down the steep stairs. They would just have to go back another time.

Emily and Zachary went to the library ahead of Aunt Risi. Emily stopped so suddenly that Zachary almost ran into her.

"Look at this, Zachary. This is what I mean. This is the article from 1940 about the daughter, Gabriella Louise Calibeary, arguing with her father and being banned from here. I put this away in the family file, but whenever I come here, it's back on the desk."

"Are you sure Aunt Risi didn't put it there."

"We both read it and agreed it should be put in the family file."

"What was the argument about?" Zachary asked.

"Her engagement," Emily said. "Her father didn't want her to marry Stephen Hadley, so they eloped, and her father banned her from this house. Emily put the article back in the file just as Aunt Risi came in. Emily turned to put a book back on the shelf when another article fell to the floor.

"Stephen and Gabriella Hadley announce the birth of their son, Jacob Stephen Hadley, December 20, 1941," Emily read. "Joseph Calibeary may have banned Gabriella from the mansion, but he still kept track of her," Emily said as she placed the new article in the family file.

After two hours, Emily and Zachary were ready for a break and convinced Aunt Risi to let them get a cold drink and take Sheba out for a quick run.

"Doesn't she ever get tired?" Zach asked as they walked to the kitchen.

"Never. She loses all track of time. It is very interesting. I get caught up too, but I usually remember to eat. Let's go outside." Emily said as soon as Sheba had a drink.

They raced out to the rose arbor with Sheba happily running and barking after them.

"We have to get back upstairs," Emily said as they laid on the grass in the sunshine. "I've been thinking about the layout. The two bedrooms facing the front are exactly the same so you would think the two bedrooms facing the back would be the same, but they're not, one is smaller. That is where we have to look."

"Gee, I never noticed that," Zachary said.

Emily felt pretty smug and was about to say so when Aunt Risi called them from the back door.

When they walked back into the library, they were all speechless as they stared at the top of the desk. The family file, open to the article about the birth of Jacob, was staring at them.

"Are you sure you put it away?" Aunt Risi asked. "Yes," Emily said. "Zachary saw me."

Zachary nodded in agreement, still speechless.

Sheba kept sniffing the air and whining as though a scent lingered but wasn't strong enough to follow.

"We may have to bury a dishrag outside the library window," Aunt Risi said.

Emily saw the look on Zachary's face and grinned. She moved closer to the desk, and the article fell to the floor. She bent over to pick it up and felt a cold draft. The article seemed to blow under the desk. She crawled under the desk and sat down. "There's a paper sticking out of a crack in the bottom of the drawer," she said. She gently pulled the paper as Aunt Risi, and Zachary crouched to watch. It was a pretty slow process, but Emily finally got the paper out and handed it to Aunt Risi.

"It's a death notice," Aunt Risi said. "Gabriella Hadley, November 24, 1943.

"What else does it say?" Emily asked.

"Stephen Hadley is taking his son Jacob, to his family home in Connecticut to live and to recuperate from their tragic loss."

"Well, that's the end of that," Emily said. "How will we ever find out anything more about this family?"

"Every state has to keep birth, marriage and death records," Aunt Risi said. "All we have to do is find the name of the town, or county in Connecticut where the Hadley family home is, or was, and we can find out what happened to Stephen and Jacob. Besides I really believe someone wants us to find them."

"How will we find the county or town?" Zachary asked.

"First, we keep looking here. There may be a letter with an address or another article with more information. After all, old Joseph saved everything else, and we still have much to search through in this room alone. I think we'll find just what we need, especially since someone is trying to help us."

Emily and Zachary just looked at each other as they pulled out a desk drawer and sat down. They searched for what seemed like hours, and they were both ready to give up when Emily squealed.

"It's from Connecticut," she said, holding an envelope in the air.

"Mystic, Connecticut." She quickly pulled the letter out and started reading.

"It's from Stephen. He wanted Joseph to know where his grandson lived. I wonder if he ever got in touch with him."

"Let's hear what Stephen has to say," Aunt Risi said.

So, Emily read Stephen's words. "Dear Mr. Calibeary, I felt I should bring Jacob to a place where he would be surrounded by people who love him. Hadley Hall is just such a place. He will be very happy here. I wanted to be sure he would be looked after in case something should happen to me, for you see I have not been well for some time. I want you to feel free to write or visit Jacob any time, even after I am no longer here. My family will welcome you."

"That was very nice of him considering Joseph's attitude about their marriage," Emily said.

"Yes, it was," Aunt Risi said. "This is just what we need to start tracking Jacob. Why don't you two take a break. I still have time to make some phone calls before the records office closes. I think we need to get to the bottom of this and soon."

Emily and Zachary wasted no time. With Sheba at their heels, they raced to the third floor and into the smaller back bedroom.

"There has to be a secret door, or maybe a whole wall moves," Emily said. "Come on Sheba, help me."

"There's a hollow sound," Zachary said as he knocked on the wall.

They searched every inch of the wall but couldn't find anything that would move. Sheba sniffed around a little and then sat down to watch.

Emily moved inside the closet only to return a few minutes later. "Nothing in there," she said. "I still think we are on the right track. The way to the tower has to be behind that wall. Could we have to go lower to find an opening, like maybe to the second floor?"

"Great idea," Zachary said as he ran toward the stairs.

"Wait! You can't go charging down there. What if Aunt Risi sees you? Besides, we need a plan,"

"Why do we always have to have a plan?"

Emily just glared at Zachary as she walked over to the window. "Help me open this shutter. I want to see which way this faces so we can be sure we pick the right room when we get downstairs."

Together, they got the shutter open and looked out of the window. A vine-covered cottage peeked out from the edge of the woods. The vines seemed to go on forever, partially covering a charming little gazebo that sat kitty-corner from the cottage.

"I wonder if that belongs to this house?" Zachary said.

"I don't know, but we will definitely check it out later. Let's go down quietly, and make sure Aunt Risi isn't in the hall before you open the door.

To their surprise, the room with the same view was the one Zachary would be using.

"If there is an opening it has to be in the closet," Emily said as they stepped inside.

"That's it," Emily said as they both looked up at the trap door in the ceiling. "Our portal to the tower."

Chapter VII
Inside the Tower

"The ceiling is too high. We can't get up there," Zachary said.

"Why does everything have to be impossible to you?"

"Well, it is awfully high." Zachary said.

"If you're afraid, I'll go by myself," Emily said as she marched off to find something to climb on.

"I'm not afraid," Zachary said, following Emily around the room.

"Then what's the problem?" Emily asked, stopping so suddenly that Zachary ran into her. Emily scowled at him, picked up a chair, and carried it to the closet.

"I just think we should tell Aunt Risi," he said.

"If we tell Aunt Risi, she will have the place crawling with police, and we don't stand a chance of finding any more clues."

"I think she would want to help us. After all, she's trying really hard to track down some members of the Calibeary family.

"That has nothing to do with this," Emily said. "If she knew I saw a Face in the window, she would call the police and probably move us out of here."

"Maybe that's what should happen. Do you ever think about the danger? What if the face you saw belongs to a criminal? What if that criminal wants to hurt us."

"Sheba wouldn't let anyone hurt me."

"Sheba can't go up in the tower with you and even if she could, how do you know he wouldn't hurt Sheba."

As Emily thought this over, she stepped up on the chair, which put her eye level with the closet shelf and a giant spider. She jumped down so fast that she knocked Zachary down in the process.

"Sorry," Emily said. "The chair won't work; we need something taller."

"No, we don't. I'll help you, but if it starts to get dangerous, we have to tell Aunt Risi."

"We will," Emily said as Zachary boosted her up on the closet shelf.

To Emily's relief, the spider scurried away, so she stood up and unlocked the trap door. With a loud squeak, the trap door swung down to the shelf, revealing a ladder that went up into a tunnel.

Emily started climbing but soon backed down. "It's too dark. I can't see a thing, she said.

"Well, what did you expect?" Zachary said, jumping down from the chair. He rummaged through his bag and found a flashlight. "Here," he said, handing it up to Emily.

Emily took the flashlight and aimed it up into the opening above her.

"Oh no," she cried as she backed away.

"Now what?" Zachary asked.

"All I can see are spider webs. There are probably a ton of those huge spiders in here." Emily said.

"Come on, you're not going to let a few spiders stop you?"

Definitely not, Emily thought as she took a deep breath and started to climb, quietly hoping what she had always heard was true: spiders are more afraid of her than she is of them.

When Emily moved up the ladder, Zachary pulled himself up on the shelf and followed her into the tunnel. They climbed quietly, listening for any sounds that might be coming from the tower. When they reached the top, they stood silently. They didn't hear anything, so they pushed and pulled until the latch gave way, and they opened the trap door to the tower.

Emily was so excited her knees were shaking as she carefully climbed the last few steps. She quickly looked around. To her relief and disappointment, there was no one in the tower.

The tower was small, with windows all around. There was barely enough room for two people.

"Look at this," Emily said. "A jacket, baseball cap, empty soda cans, food wrappers and snack bags. We found our thief."

"No, we didn't," Zachary said. "He's not here, just his trail. He's probably long gone by now, but just in case he's not, I think we should get out of here."

"Not yet. Wow, look at this."

"Oh no," Zachary said as Emily opened up a small door, revealing another passageway.

"We are not going in there," Zachary said.

"We have to see where it leads," Emily said as she crawled inside, shining her light all around.

"Aunt Risi will be looking for us," Zachary said.

"It's a tunnel and it goes down," Emily said as she backed out of the small opening.

"Come on Emily. We have to get out of here."

"Okay," she said. "You're right. Aunt Risi will be looking for us. We wouldn't want her to come into your room looking for us and find the trap door. "We'll investigate this tomorrow."

Zachary was the last one down, making sure the trap door to the tower was closed and latched from the bottom. If the passage Emily found was another way into the tower, no one could come down the shaft and surprise him in his sleep. Once he got down to the closet shelf, he made sure the trap door in the closet was closed and latched before jumping down.

"Let's go see what Aunt Risi found out," Emily said as she put the chair back and closed the closet door.

Aunt Risi was just hanging up the phone as they came down the stairs into the hall.

"Mimi cancelled her flight. She's not feeling well. I'm not sure when she'll be coming," Aunt Risi said. "This always happens when she forgets to sleep with the window open when the moon is full."

"Did you find out anything about the Hadley family?" Emily asked, trying not to giggle over the full-moon comment. "I hope Mimi feels better soon," She added, remembering her manners.

"Yes, I did. There is a young boy about 14 years old. I talked with a Mr. George Hadley at Hadley Hall. He told me the boy lives with his stepfather, a Mr. Raymond Burns. Mr. Hadley couldn't or wouldn't tell me anything else. Then I remembered my friend, Irene. She lives near Mystic, so, I called her to see if she had ever heard of Mr. Burns, or perhaps knew of the Hadley family. At first, she said she didn't know them, but then she remembered seeing something in the newspaper about a Mr. Burns and his stepson. She went to find the paper and read the article to me. Jake Hadley has run away from home, and Mr. Burns is offering a reward for his return. The article said they interviewed a friend of Jake's. He said that Jake ran away because Burns was very mean and abusive to him."

"Wow," Emily said. "That means we better find him soon. Maybe we can help him."

"Irene will try to get more information for us and call back sometime tomorrow."

"When are we going to eat?" Zachary asked, as his stomach suddenly growled, reminding them all what time it was.

"Oh my," Aunt Risi said. "I've done it again. I get so carried away that I lose all track of time. Growing children need to eat. Let's go see what we can find in the kitchen.

"And tomorrow we'll see what we can find," Emily whispered to Zachary as they followed Aunt Risi.

Chapter VIII
Midnight Procession

Emily awoke from a sound sleep. Did she hear something, or was she dreaming? Sheba didn't growl or bark. In fact, Sheba was sound asleep. Emily strained her ears. She thought it must have been a dream and turned over to go back to sleep. Just as she closed her eyes, she heard the sound again, and this time Sheba heard it too. She growled softly.

"Shh," Emily said as she crept out of bed and walked toward the door.

Sheba followed Emily into the hall. They heard the sound again just as Zachary's door flew open. Emily jumped and almost tripped.

"Did you hear that?" Zachary asked.

"Yes, Emily whispered. "Listen, there it is again." She pointed down, and Zachary nodded.

"You aren't going down there," Zachary said as Emily quietly started moving toward the stairs.

She ignored him and kept walking. Aunt Risi's door suddenly opened, and they both froze in their tracks.

"What is going on?" Aunt Risi asked.

"We heard a noise from downstairs," Zachary blurted out before Emily could stop him.

"Let's investigate," Aunt Risi said and, to Emily's surprise, led the way toward the stairs. The quiet procession moved slowly in the dark hall, stopping each time they heard the noise. Aunt Risi grabbed a long silver candlestick as they started down the stairs. Halfway down the stairs, they heard the noise again. Emily was sure it was coming from the library.

Aunt Risi must have thought so too, because she turned that way when they reached the bottom of the stairs.

They crept along as silently as possible. Sheba, alert and ready, led the way. They stopped outside the library and listened. Emily could feel the hair standing up on the back of her neck, and she felt suddenly very cold. In one swift movement, Aunt Risi stepped inside the library and turned on the light. There was no one there. Sheba was acting very strange, sniffing the air and whining. They quickly checked all the main floor doors and windows and found them all closed and locked from the inside.

Sheba settled down, so they went back to the library.

Once again, the family folder was on the desk, but something new had been added this time: a map of the house and grounds.

"Someone wants us to know something," Aunt Risi said. "I just wish I knew what, because the map couldn't possibly have any connection with finding the runaway boy."

As Aunt Risi talked, Emily studied the map. It showed the cottage, the gazebo, and the entire wooded area surrounding the yard. It showed the layout of the house and a funny line, almost like a walkway or road, between the cottage and the back of the house.

Emily didn't want Aunt Risi to get too interested in the map until she had more time to study it and do some investigating. She folded it up and suggested they go to the kitchen for hot chocolate.

"I think it's a ghost," Zachary said through sips of hot chocolate.

"The ghost of Joseph Calibeary. He feels guilty because he was so mean to his daughter."

"I think it's a ghost too," Aunt Risi said. "But I think its Gabriella."

Emily couldn't believe what she was hearing. Aunt Risi calmly sitting there, discussing ghosts? She was so surprised she almost brought up the missing food. She stopped herself just in time; after all, that could make Aunt Risi see things a little differently and want to call the police.

Before Emily could think of anything to say, Aunt Risi was shooing them both off to bed. "Crawl into bed from the right side so you won't have bad dreams," she said.

Emily rolled her eyes at Zachary, and they both went to bed.

No matter how hard she tried, Emily could not fall asleep. After lying in bed for what seemed like hours, she finally gave up and went to the library to study the map.

"What could this line between the cottage and the house mean?" In answer, Sheba wagged her tail and wined a bit.

"I thought I would find you here," Zachary said from the doorway. "I couldn't sleep either."

"This map shows the tower and the shaft to the closet. It also shows the other opening from the tower out and down. Down to where, I wonder?"

"It just stops."

"Why don't you ask Aunt Risi," Zachary said. "She was pretty cool last night. She didn't even think about calling the police."

"I know, but that's because she thinks our intruder is a ghost."

"Oh, and you don't? How do you suppose someone got in here when all the doors and windows are locked from the inside?" Zachary said.

"I don't know that yet, but I will," Emily said.

"Why don't you think it's a ghost?"

"Because of the disappearing food. And don't forget the jacket, and cap we found in the tower." Emily thought for a moment as she studied the map. Suddenly, her expression changed as another idea came to her.

'What?" Zachary asked as he saw her eyes light up.

"What if we have more than one intruder? One ghostly, leaving clues about the family all over the place, and one not so ghostly, eating our food."

Zachary thought this over. "That would explain a lot, but I still don't see how anyone could get in here without breaking a lock or window or something.

"There has to be a way. Come on, let's take Sheba out and we'll have a look at the cottage by the woods."

The sun was just coming up as they went out. The cottage was quite a distance from the house. If there was a path, it was overgrown long ago, with no visible signs that it ever existed, they had to walk through tall weeds and crawl under low branches. Sheba thought this was great fun and ran circles around them as she sniffed out the area.

"So much for the map." Emily said.

As they inched closer to the cottage, Sheba stopped and growled *softly. She sniffed the air and the ground before following the trail of* something or someone right up to the cottage door. She stood guarding the door, growling softly, her hair standing on her back.

"Maybe we shouldn't go in," Zachary whispered.

For once, Emily seemed to think Zachary was right. She crouched down in the weeds, pulling him down with her.

"Follow me," she whispered and started crawling toward the side of the cottage. They crouched below the window and listened for any sounds coming from inside the cottage. Emily couldn't hear anything, so she pointed to the window and slowly stood up enough to peek inside.

At first, she couldn't see anything, but as she shaded her eyes, she could see someone asleep in the corner.

"I think we may have found the owner of the jacket and cap we found in the tower," Emily whispered, as she knelt down next to Zachary.

"Do you think we should go in?" Zachary asked.

"We have to. Sheba will take care of us," Emily said. They crawled to the front of the cottage, where Sheba was standing guard by the door.

Emily quietly opened the door; Sheba inched her way inside, the hair raised on her back and her teeth barred.

Chapter IX
A Secret

Emily and Zachary slowly and carefully followed Sheba inside. Sheba was standing on the intruder's chest, growling, and the intruder was frozen in terror.

"Who are you and what are you doing here?" Zachary yelled. "That should show him whose boss," Emily said, staring at the boy in the corner.

"Call your dog off!"

"I will as soon as you tell us who you are," Emily said.

"I'm Jake Hadley. Now call your dog off!".

Emily and Zachary both stood, mouths open, staring.

"Jake Hadley, from Mystic Connecticut?" Emily asked. "Down Sheba."

"How do you know about me?" Jake asked.

"Aunt Risi told us. She said you ran away from home," Zachary said.

"Who's Aunt Risi?"

"She's our Great Aunt and the new owner of Calibeary Manor," Emily said.

"So, my stepfather really did sell this place. Is that how she knew about me, from my stepfather?"

"No, Aunt Risi bought this place from the realtor. She never heard of you or your stepfather until we all came here."

"You can't tell anyone that I'm here,' Jake said. I don't want my stepfather to find me."

"We have to tell, you're too young to be on your own. Besides, Aunt Risi will help you. She knows who you are and that you are a member of the Calibeary family," Zachary said.

"No one can help me."

"You sure left a lot of clues for someone who didn't want to be found," Emily said.

"What are you talking about"?

"All the stuff in the library."

"I have never been in the library." Jake said.

"Oh right, and I suppose you have never been in the kitchen, or in the Tower either," Zachary said.

"Yes, I was in the kitchen, and I was in the tower, but that's all."

"I was fine here until you came."

"Oh really, and what were you eating?" Zachary asked.

"I was getting kind of hungry," Jake admitted. "I was pretty happy when I saw that man and woman bring in bags of stuff and then leave."

"So, you admit you were stealing our food," Emily said.

"Yes, I stole some food, but that's all. Look, I'll be gone in a few days. Please don't tell anyone I'm here."

"We have to tell," Zachary said. "Besides, where will you go?

You can't just keep running."

"I know, but I don't have a better plan right now."

"Okay," Emily said. "We don't blame you for stealing the food, but how did you get in?"

"Through the tunnel."

"What tunnel?" Emily asked.

"The one that's underneath that trap door over there," Jake said as he pointed to the other corner.

"The walkway on the map," Emily said. "Where does it lead?"

"You can get up to the tower, or you can go through the cellar and upstairs to the kitchen. I haven't gone to the tower since you got here, and I've only been to the kitchen late at night.

"Your jacket and hat are in the tower." Zachary said.

"I know. That and the food are the only reason I haven't moved on."

"How did you happen to come here?" Emily asked.

"My dad, my real dad, always told me stories about his grandmother living here. He said someday we would live here and that this place would be mine. I just wanted to see it and then move on, but then I stayed until I could figure out what to do next. I just happened to find the tunnel by accident, that's how I ended up in the tower and saw you driving away."

"Someone wanted us to find you," Emily said. "And that someone knows you are here."

"What do you mean?"

"We'd better go back to the house. Aunt Risi will be looking for us," Zachary said. "Besides, it's time for breakfast," he added, his stomach growling.

"Zachary's right," Emily said. "She'll be worried after what happened last night."

"What happened last night?"

"A noise from the library woke us up, so we all went to investigate."

"When we got there, we found a map of the house and grounds on the desk." Emily said.

"Was someone in the house?"

"That's just it," Emily and Zachary said together.

"No one was there, and all the doors and windows were locked from the inside. Besides, Sheba would have been able to track an intruder. We'll come back as soon as we can," Zachary said. "We won't tell for now, and we'll try to bring you some food."

"Thanks, that would be great," Jake said.

"That was nice of you," Emily said. "You were pretty brave too."

"Thanks," Zachary said with a look of total surprise.

They found Aunt Risi in the kitchen. She was dressed in her Austrian Mountain climbing outfit. Zachary started to laugh, but Emily poked him just as Aunt Risi turned to look at them. '

"We took Sheba out for a run," Emily said. "She's been inside a lot since we got here."

"I think we should all spend some time outside today. We could use some fresh air and exercise," Zachary said.

"Yes," Aunt Risi said, her eyes twinkling. "We have been working pretty hard. I keep forgetting that young people need to blow off steam once in a while, or you'll boil over. How would you like a picnic?"

"That would be great," Zachary said.

"Oh dear, I just remembered I'm expecting some very important phone calls. But you can still go. No sense in all of us being cooped up here. We'll get everything ready after breakfast. Just remember to turn all the way around and take three steps backward if you see an owl on the ground or in a tree."

"Nice work, Zachary," Emily said as they ran upstairs to wash up and change for breakfast. "We can take Jake some food and explore the tunnel."

"Wow," Zachary said. "Two compliments in one day. Are you feeling alright Miss Em?"

Emily thought about that, and it suddenly dawned on her that she had meant both of those compliments. It also suddenly dawned on her that Zachary really is pretty nice and maybe not so weird after all. Perhaps she was just too quick to judge. Oh well, no time to worry about that now. They had a picnic lunch to pack and some very important exploring to do.

Chapter X
The Secret Passage

With a huge picnic lunch in hand, Emily and Zachary wished Aunt Risi good luck with her phone calls and went outside. Sheba led the way, her tail wagging in her excitement to be going outside.

"I'm glad we're going out. It's much too nice to be stuck indoors," Emily said as they waved to Aunt Risi.

"Maybe we should go out back and around the rose trellis so Aunt Risi won't know we're going to the potter's cottage," Zachary said.

"Okay," Emily said. "But I don't know if she even knows it's there. Besides, you can't even see it from the house except from your bedroom window and the third floor."

Sheba was so happy to be free that she ran ahead of them, sniffing the ground. It was a longer trek but a little easier as they made their way around the trellis and through the back gate. They walked along the edge of the woods and pretty soon spotted the back of the cottage. Sheba ran ahead, playfully barking at the squirrels and birds. They walked between the gazebo and the cottage and approached the door, where they found Jake waiting for them.

"I heard Sheba barking. How did you manage to get back here so soon and with food?" Jake asked as Emily handed him a sandwich. "Gee thanks, I'm starving."

"Zachary told Aunt Risi we needed an outing, and she agreed. She even helped us pack a picnic lunch," Emily said. "She had to stay in because she was expecting some phone calls."

"How did you get all the way here from Connecticut?" Zachary asked.

"I heard my stepfather and his brother Carl talking about picking up some horses. Carl said he was going to Berger family farms in Berlin Heights. I remembered Calibeary Manor was in Berlin Heights. I could only hope that it was the same Berlin Heights, but even if it wasn't I knew I couldn't stay with my stepfather any longer, so I decided to take my chances. I hid in the storage compartment in the bottom of the trailer. When we got to Burger Farms I rolled out of the trailer and hid until Carl loaded the horses and drove away. After that I walked a lot, mostly at night. I was hiding in a tree line that divided two fields and a farmer came to work the ground. I was afraid he would see me, so I practically crawled through the tree line into the woods. I ran through the woods and ended up across the road from here. I couldn't believe my eyes when I read the sign over the front gate, Calibeary Manor. I came around back and found this cottage. I was really tired, so I came inside and slept. It's not much, but at least it's a roof over my head," Jake said.

"Aren't you scared?" Emily asked.

"Yes, but I came this far. I'll be okay."

"How did you find the tunnel?" Emily asked as she looked around the cluttered room.

Flowerpots filled one corner, and large burlap sacks covered most of the floor. A potting table covered one whole wall, with gardening tools hanging all around the edges. Window boxes stood stacked along the front wall, and shovels, rakes, and hoes filled the corner behind the door.

The only window was above the potting table, giving just enough light.

"I got kind of cold that first night so I picked up some of the burlap sacks to cover up with. The next morning, I saw the trap door."

"I brought the map from the library," Emily said. "Let's explore the tunnel."

"Okay," Jake said. "Did you bring a flashlight?"

"Yes," Zachary said. "What did you use."

"I have a flashlight, but the batteries are getting really weak." Jake said.

"We'll get you some new ones. Let's get going," Emily said.

After ensuring the cottage door was closed tight and braced with a rake, Jake opened the trap door. Narrow stone steps led the way down into the dark, damp tunnel. Jake went down first using his dim light. Emily and Sheba followed. Emily shivered a little as she descended into the cold, eerie tunnel. Zachary was last, shining his bright light all around as he reached the bottom step.

"Wow," Emily said as she started forward.

"Are you sure it's safe down here?" Zachary asked as he pulled Emily back to the step.

"Everything seems pretty solid," Jake said. "I checked it out when my light was still bright. They used lots of beams and huge quarry stones to reinforce the beams."

They slowly started walking into the black tunnel. They could only see a short distance ahead, even with the bright light. Emily, still shivering, followed the beams of light, watching for spiders or any other unpleasant creature that might be lurking in the tunnel. Sheba led the way, sniffing as she went, stopping occasionally to let Emily, Zachary, and Jake catch up.

"Wow, this is unbelievable," Emily said. "Who could have built this and why would they need it?"

"I don't know," Jake said. "My dad probably didn't know anything about the tunnel and secret passages because he never told me.

Of course, I was only seven when he died."

"Maybe we'll find out if we keep searching the library. We haven't had time to look for anything else since we found the map. We don't even know for sure when this place was built," Emily said.

"It was in the eighteen hundreds, right before the civil war," Jake said.

"At least that's what I remember my dad telling me."

Large wooden beams were placed evenly along the walls and across the top of the tunnel, with huge quarry stone pillars holding up the center beams. Old-fashioned lanterns were placed along one side to light the way of long-ago visitors. An occasional mouse scurried out of their path, and there were a few spider webs, but Emily was too excited to care.

They walked along for what seemed like a long time.

"We're getting close to the house," Jake said. "We have to be really quiet. The entrance is in the back of the coal bin, and we have to crawl through the opening. Once we get there, No talking."

Zachary's flashlight revealed a stone wall. Jake pointed his dim beam of light to a low, square door near the dirt floor of the tunnel.

"How did you ever find this," Emily whispered.

Jake shrugged and bent to open the door. One by one, they slipped through into the coal bin. Jake then opened a normal-sized door that led into a huge cellar. There was some broken-down furniture in one corner and a coal furnace along the back wall. Floor-to-ceiling cabinets had been built under the stairs and continued to the side wall. Everything was coated with a thick layer of dust and decorated in giant spider webs like the rest of the house.

"The stairs go up into the pantry in the kitchen," Jake whispered.

"How do you get to the tower?" Emily whispered.

Jake opened a cabinet door. At first, it just looked like a cabinet, but Jake pushed on a board in the back wall, and it opened up, revealing a ladder.

Emily crawled inside and looked up. It was awfully dark, but she could see all the way up the ladder with the flashlight. She climbed cautiously, looking for spiders, when Jake grabbed her leg.

"Your aunt will hear us," he whispered. "Let's go back."

Even though she knew Jake was right, Emily was disappointed that her investigation had been cut short.

Making sure the cupboard doors were closed, they quietly slipped back into the tunnel.

"That was amazing. I have just got to find out why they needed secret passages," Emily said as they followed the tunnel back to the cottage.

Maybe we'll find something in the library, or maybe Aunt Risi knows something about all of this," Zachary said.

"Maybe, but I don't think we should ask her, at least not yet," Emily said as they climbed the steps into the cottage. "For now, let's eat lunch."

"Let's go out into the woods, Jake could use the fresh air."

Outside was all Sheba needed to hear. She raced up the last few steps and waited by the door, tail wagging.

They went out between the cottage and the gazebo and into the woods. They walked along, enjoying the warm breeze and sunspots through the trees until they came across a small clearing. Someone had made a table out of a large tree stump, and smaller chunks of logs made the seats.

"This is perfect," Emily said as Zachary helped her spread the tablecloth. Sheba chased the birds and squirrels while they ate their lunch.

"Why did you run away?" Emily asked.

"You would have run away too if you had a stepfather like Raymond Burns," Jake said. "He's mean and greedy. When my father died seven years ago, my mom inherited all of the Calibeary fortune, including this estate. She put everything in a trust fund for me. This house was supposed to be part of it. About four years ago, my mom met Raymond. He seemed nice and spent a lot of time with me until they got married. Then he changed; he was suspicious of everything. He questioned my mother about where she went and who she talked to, and it kept getting worse. Before long, he wouldn't let her leave the house without him or one of his thugs. He would rant and rave and question her until she cried. When she died, he started on me."

"For the past two years, he has controlled everything I have done. He even had a tutor come last semester so he wouldn't have to send me to school. He wouldn't let me see my friends or go anywhere. He said he had control of my trust fund, and if I told anyone, he would sell this house, and I wouldn't have anything."

Emily's eyes filled with tears, but she looked away so the boys couldn't see her. She didn't want anyone to think she was soft.

"We'll find a way to help you," Zachary said, "I know Aunt Risi will do everything she can."

"Just don't tell her I'm here," Jake said. "My own family hasn't helped me, why should she?"

"We promised we wouldn't tell," Emily said as she packed up the trash and handed Jake the extra sandwich for supper. "But we can't just let you leave. You could end up worse off. There are some very scary people out there."

"I'll think of something," Jake said as they walked back to the potter's cottage.

"We better get back, we'll bring you some food tomorrow," Emily said. "Maybe Aunt Risi has some news."

Chapter XI
News From Hadley Hall

Emily, Zachary, and Sheba raced along the path and around the trellis to find Aunt Risi waiting for them by the back door. She was holding a shovel.

"What's up?" Zachary asked as they came to a stop.

"I decided it would be a good idea to plant a potato wrapped in a dishrag under the library window. I was planning to do it earlier, but I've had a very exciting day," Aunt Risi said. "Let's go inside where we can talk."

They followed Aunt Risi inside and into the library. Once seated, Aunt Rise said, "First, my friend Irene called. She said she heard on the news that Mr. Burns had a detective looking for Jake Hadley."

Emily and Zachary looked at each other, and Aunt Risi continued.

"Then my realtor called. He said someone from Hadley Hall wanted to know how to reach me. The realtor said he didn't want to give out my number but he would give me the message. I no sooner hung up and the phone rang again. This time it was Raymond Burns. He told me it would be best for all concerned if I didn't talk with anyone from Hadley Hall. He said, they did not get along and did not approve of the sale of Calibeary Manor."

"Wow," Emily said. "Then what?"

"I called Hadley Hall. No one is going to tell me who I can talk to."

"What did they want?" Zachary asked.

"Well, Jake has another relative. His mother's sister Lora. She wants custody of Jake but Burns threatened to harm him if Lora interfered. Now that Jake has run away, she is pushing very hard for custody and has hired her own private detective to find him. She is also trying to get the police to investigate some of the business deals Burns is involved in. She believes that he sold this house to me illegally. She said she is pretty sure this house was part of the trust fund set up by Jake's mother before she married Mr. Burns. She also said she would make sure Burns could never hurt Jake again."

"What do we do now?" Emily asked.

"Well, Lora thinks maybe Jake will turn up here. He probably doesn't know Burns sold the manor."

"Do you think the detectives will come here?" Zachary asked, not looking at Aunt Risi.

"Eventually, but I think we have some time before that happens. We need to keep our eyes and ears open. Maybe we can find Jake and save him from any more heartbreak. He's suffered enough."

"What about Calibeary Manor?" Emily asked. "Do we have to leave?"

"I don't know yet. Of course, I want to do the right thing, we'll just have to wait and see what the right thing is."

Emily and Zachary looked at each other. They really needed to talk, but getting away now wouldn't be easy, not after being gone all day. They promised Jake they wouldn't tell, but Aunt Risi only wants to help. Emily needed time to think.

"Let's go into the parlor," Aunt Risi said. "I found an old phonograph and some records. Let's crank it up and see what it sounds like."

They listened to songs that were popular in the forties while Aunt Risi sang along and danced a little.

"Come dance with me," Aunt Risi said.

At first, they wouldn't get up, but she wouldn't take no for an answer and pulled them both to their feet. They were soon dancing and laughing and having a wonderful time. Sheba joined in the fun, jumping around and barking at them.

Even though they were having so much fun, Emily couldn't get Jake off her mind. We just have to convince him to let us tell Aunt Risi she thought.

The fun continued until Zachary announced, "I am so hungry that my stomach is touching my backbone."

"How about homemade pizza?" Aunt Risi asked.

"Sounds great," Emily and Zachary said, racing to the kitchen. Aunt Risi fixed the dough while Emily and Zachary got the pans ready. Then they piled on the sauce, pepperoni, and cheese and were getting ready to put it in the oven when they noticed Aunt Risi putting seaweed, tofu, and bean sprouts on hers. With wrinkled noses, they popped them in the oven and ran upstairs to get cleaned up while the pizza baked.

"I wish Jake could have some," Emily said.

"He could if we tell Aunt Risi," Zachary said.

"We can't," Emily said. "We promised. Besides, we need to ask Jake about his Aunt Lora before we can decide what to do."

After they stuffed themselves with pizza, they went back to the parlor.

Emily picked up a book from the coffee table. "Spooky tales," she read. "Should we read some?"

Aunt Risi and Zachary agreed, so they took turns reading scary stories about ghosts and goblins, haunted houses, and cemeteries until bedtime. Emily had to admit to herself that staying here with Aunt Risi and Zachary was way more fun than she ever thought.

"How are we going to get out in the morning?" Zachary asked as they climbed up the stairs.

"We'll have to go really early," Emily said. "Whoever wakes up first gets the other one up."

"Okay, see you in the morning."

Emily crawled into her sleeping bag. It had been another very busy day, and she was exhausted. Sheba must have been very tired, too, because they were both asleep in no time. It was a cloudy night, and Emily's room was very dark. Her eyes suddenly opened, but she didn't know what woke her. She couldn't hear anything, but she had a feeling she should get up.

She went to the window and looked down at the backyard. It was very dark, but she thought she saw something moving. With Sheba at her side, she quickly went to Zachary's room.

"I think someone's outside," she whispered.

They both looked out Zachary's window. It was so dark they could barely see the roof of the cottage.

"There, did you see it? Something moved," Emily said. They kept watching and saw it again.

"It's not Jake."

"You're right," Zachary said. "Let's get Aunt Risi."

For once, Emily didn't argue, and they ran to Aunt Risi's room. "Aunt Risi, wake up, someone's outside," Emily said.

They all ran to the window but didn't see anything. They ran to Zachary's window, and still nothing.

"Are you sure you saw something?" Aunt Risi asked as she peered into the darkness.

"Positive," they both said at once.

They crept downstairs, and together, they peered into the darkness.

Nothing moved. They watched and waited, and still nothing moved.

"If you're sure you saw something, we should call the police," Aunt Risi said.

Emily and Zachary were very worried. What if something had happened to Jake. What if someone found him. They looked at each other and silently agreed the time had come to tell Aunt Risi.

"What's the matter with you two?" Aunt Risi asked. "You both look very worried."

"We are," Emily said. "We have to tell you something, but you better sit down. Jake Hadley is here," she blurted out.

"What? Here? At Calibeary Manor?" Aunt Risi asked, looking at them both with eyebrows raised and a worried frown on her forehead.

"Yes, well, not inside," Emily said, swallowing. "He's in the potter's cottage."-

"We don't know who's out there," Zachary said. "What if it's the detective his stepfather hired?"

"It could be, but whoever it is, they have no business on this property," Aunt Risi said, standing up, ready to take action. "Until some decisions are made, I am still the owner. Let's go get him."

"Wait, there's a better way," Emily said as she took a deep breath. "If there is someone out there and they haven't already found Jake, we don't want to let them know he's here."

"You're right, Emily, but what else can we do?" Aunt Risi asked.

"We'll go through the secret passage. Get your flashlight, Zachary," Emily said.

"What secret passage?" Aunt Risi asked, sitting down again.

"You'll see," Emily said as Zachary returned with the flashlight.

"I think I'd better call the police. If we run into trouble at least they'll be on their way."

When Aunt Risi hung up the phone, Emily grabbed her hand and quickly led her into the pantry, down the basement stairs, and into the coal bin.

Chapter XII
A FinalVisit

"You two have been very busy," Aunt Risi said when she found her voice.

Inside the coal bin, Zachary bent to open the small door. He went through first, followed by Sheba, Aunt Risi, and Emily.

"How did you find this, and when did you have time?" Aunt Risi asked with sheer wonder in her voice.

"Jake showed us today," Emily said. "It's on the map too. It goes to the potter's cottage."

"We have a lot to talk about, but not here, we wouldn't want anyone to hear us."

They traveled silently, listening for any sound coming from above them. Suddenly, Emily grabbed Aunt Risi's arm. "Listen," she whispered, pointing up. "Voices." But exactly where were the voices coming from.

Please don't let them find Jake, Emily thought. Zachary was right; we should have told Aunt Risi sooner. After what seemed like a very long walk, they finally reached the steps leading to the trap door. They paused, straining their ears. At first, they heard nothing, then they heard men's voices again.

Were they inside the cottage? Emily was so nervous she was shaking. She could only hope that Jake was still there.

Zachary turned off his flashlight and slowly started pushing up on the trap door. Oh, please let Jake be there, Emily thought. Suddenly, the trap door opened, and someone jumped in, almost on top of Zachary.

Zachary lost his balance and nearly knocked Emily off the steps. The trap door closed almost as fast as it opened, and Zachary turned his flashlight back on to shine on the new arrival. It was Jake.

"Are you okay?" Emily whispered.

"Yes. What are you doing here? You're going to get caught for sure," Jake said.

"We saw someone outside," Emily said as she breathed a sigh of relief. "We were worried about you. I am so glad you're safe."

"There is someone outside. My stepfather's thugs are here. I heard them talking, so I braced the door and hid." Jake whispered.

"We decided we better tell Aunt Risi," Emily whispered.

"No, don't do that. I'll be gone soon," Jake whispered, reaching up to latch the trap door shut.

"We've already told her," Zachary whispered as Aunt Risi moved closer to the light.

"I'm not going back. I'm never going back," Jake said softly.

"It's okay Jake, we're on your side. Aunt Risi is too. She has a lot to tell you," Zachary whispered.

"Yes, I do, but this is not the place. Let's go back to the house, where we are all safe and a little warmer," Aunt Risi whispered. "I think we all have a lot to say. Right Emily?"

"Yes, Aunt Risi," Emily said, smiling somewhat sheepishly.

"Don't worry, Jake," Emily said as Jake pulled back. "Everything will be okay," She added, silently hoping everything would be okay for all of them.

It was a silent group that Sheba led back through the secret passage. They filed up the stairs one by one, through the pantry, and into the kitchen.

In no time at all, they were seated at the table with steaming mugs of Valerian tea in front of them. Sheba, relieved to finally have them all in the same room, sat between Emily and Jake.

"As much as I want to hear everything you have been up to, I think I should go first," Aunt Risi said. "Did you know your Aunt Lora has been trying to get custody of you?"

"No," Jake said. "My stepfather hasn't let me see any of my family since my mother died."

"I talked with Lora yesterday. She said your stepfather threatened to harm you if she tried to take you away from him. She was afraid he would follow through with his threat, so she sat back and waited, hoping something would change. When she heard that you had run away, she hired a private detective to find you and then immediately filed for custody."

"I didn't think anyone cared," Jake said.

"Well, she does and so does Mr. Hadley. They were just too afraid for your safety, but before this goes any further, she wants to make sure it's what you want," Aunt Risi said. "Should we call her?"

"Yes, that would be great," Jake said.

Aunt Risi and Jake went to make the call, returning a few minutes later. Jake looked relieved and a lot happier.

"Aunt Lora is on her way," Jake said. "And guess what else. My stepfather has been arrested for being involved in illegal activities."

"Part of which was selling this house," Aunt Risi said.

"What about you, Aunt Risi?" Emily asked, realizing she did not want Aunt Risi to move away.

"This house belongs to Jake and that's as it should be. I'll stop final payment and I will get the rest back in time. The realtor and the bank will help me. Now, I want to hear all about your adventure and how you found Jake."

With Zachary's help, Emily told Aunt Risi the whole story, starting with seeing the face in the tower window on the very first day she visited the house. They were interrupted by a knock on the door. It was a policeman letting them know that they had seen a lot of large footprints around the house and the potter's cottage. They didn't see anyone around, but a patrol car will remain in the area for the rest of the night. Then Emily finished her story.

"How exciting," Aunt Risi said.

"You aren't mad at us, well mainly me, for not telling you?" Emily asked, very surprised.

"It would have been fun to have been included in all the excitement and you did take some chances, but I'm not angry. Don't forget, we shared some pretty exciting midnight visits," Aunt Risi said.

"That's right," Emily said. "We all helped to solve this mystery in some way. Even our midnight visitor."

"Yes," Aunt Risi said. "That's one part we may never stop puzzling over."

"May, I see the library?" Jake asked.

"Of course, you may," Aunt Risi said. "It is your house, after all."

They went into the library, and there on the desk was the family file. They exchanged looks and moved a little closer to the desk. The file included a book about the Underground Railroad, three gold coins from the Civil War, and an old picture of a very pretty young woman. She was holding a baby and smiling. The room, for the first time, seemed warm and cozy. The cold, damp feeling was gone.

"That's my great grandmother," Jake said. "Gabriella Louise Calibeary Hadley."

"She can rest now," Aunt Risi said as she put her arms around Emily and Zachary, confident that the last piece of the puzzle had been solved.

"Jake is safe, and all has been put right."

"Not everything Aunt Risi. What are you going to do? You won't move away again, will you?" Emily asked.

"Maybe we should all get some rest. It looks like starting tomorrow, we will be doing some house hunting," Aunt Risi said, hugging her niece and nephew.

"I can't wait," Emily said, hugging Aunt Risi back. And I don't care what outfit she wears, Emily thought as she went upstairs to bed, happy knowing that her best friend, Zachary, felt the same way.

MYSTERY AT QUARTER BAR FARM

A J Witt.

Chapter I
A Home for Aunt Risi

"Oh, Aunt Risi this is it," Emily exclaimed from the rumble seat of Aunt Risi's English Roadster.

"It is," Kathy, Emily's Mom said. "It's remote, and peaceful here. The house is almost as big and almost as old as Calibeary Manor. If the inside is as enchanting as the outside, I think our search is over. It's still in Berlin Heights, so it's close and it may very well have an interesting past."

They were sitting at the end of the driveway looking at the old Quarter Bar Farm Mansion, just a few miles from the village of Berlin Heights, Ohio.

"The owners of Quarter Bar Farms, the Pond family, just put this house on the market yesterday." Aunt Risi said. "The current Quarter Bar Farm Mansion is about a mile down the road. The realtor told me that this mansion has eight bedrooms and six bathrooms, so there is plenty of room for my nieces and nephews and all of my old and new friends to come to visit me."

Aunt Risi drove up to the house and parked the car. Emily and Sheba, her Black Lab jumped out of the rumble seat and ran up the steps as Aunt Risi and Mom followed a little slower and unlocked the front door. Sheba was excited and ran into the house ahead of them sniffing the air. They all followed Sheba inside and then just stood as they saw the beautiful ornate great hall and grand open stairway.

The wide stairway stood in the very middle of the front hall with the railing curving out at the bottom on both sides. At the top of the stairs, the ornate railing continued along both sides to form a kind of balcony. They all just stood there, speechless for a few minutes until Aunt Risi found her voice.

"Well," Aunt Risi said. "I don't think enchanting quite covers this. I am so very surprised at the beauty and character of the entry hall alone. Let's look at the rest."

They were all drawn to the stairs, so they went up and found a little sitting room in the open area at the top with a hallway leading off in each direction. To the left, they found a very large master bedroom with a private bath and a large, walk-in closet. There was another big bedroom with its own bath across the hall and more bedrooms and bathrooms at the other end of the hall. The Pond family had left some furniture, but there was plenty of room for all of Aunt Risi's stuff.

They headed back downstairs and walked through the first-floor rooms. There was a parlor, a large office that was fully furnished, and a large dining room with an archway that led to the huge kitchen. There was also a big family room with a fireplace that Emily could stand up in, a small library and another bedroom and bathroom.

"This room will be perfect for Mimi when she comes." Aunt Risi said. "I think this house is perfect for me."

Yes, Emily thought, Mimi, Aunt Risi's ancient housekeeper would be happy not to have to climb stairs. In truth, Mimi doesn't do much housekeeping anymore. It's more like Aunt Risi takes care of Mimi now.

Emily, dressed in jean shorts and a red softball jersey, her blond windblown hair tucked into a baseball cap, wandered into the office and sat at the big desk. "This, kind of reminds me of Calibeary Manor," She, said to Sheba. She opened the desk drawer and found a very old police report. It said the house had been robbed and several valuable pieces of jewelry and some old gold coins were taken.

"Well, this is very interesting," she said to Sheba. "I wonder if they ever found the person who did this and if they ever found the missing valuables. We'll have to see what we can find out after all this time."

"Let's go outside," Mom called from the kitchen. "I want to see the grounds and the view."

Outside was all Sheba needed to hear. She ran out the back door as soon as it was opened. They found the grounds to be quite extensive and in need of some tender loving care, but still quite beautiful.

"Oh, look, Aunt Risi," Emily said, her big blue eyes shining. "It's a gazebo and a patio and a fire pit. Oh, and a place to cook. I love this place. And look out there," she pointed, "a barn and I see some fences. Maybe you can get some horses. How much land do you have here?"

'Slow down a bit Emily," Mom said, looking pretty with her long dark hair and brown eyes. "I wonder why they ever built a new house. I would have never left this beautiful place. I would have never moved out."

"Well, we probably should find out," Aunt Risi said. "And also, why it's been sitting empty for all these years. I am thankful they kept up with all the necessary repairs, but I do have some questions. I suppose I can get some answers from the realtor, but let's drive down to the farm and maybe we'll learn something just by looking at the newer house."

They drove the mile down the road and saw a very beautiful farm. The house, really a mansion, bigger than the old mansion, was very beautiful, as were the grounds. There were several barns, paddocks, outdoor training rings, and Emily suspected, there were also indoor riding areas and training rings. To the West and South of the barns, there were acres and acres of fenced-in pasture. Emily saw a young man leading a beautiful brown horse out of the paddock into one of the training rings. It was a sight she hoped she would see again.

They drove down the road further and turned around to go past the farm again. Emily noticed lots of open land across the road. Probably for hay, Emily thought. They drove on by and then went very slowly past the old mansion.

"I'm sold," Aunt Risi said. "I want some answers, but I am ready to buy this beautiful place. Let's go see the realtor."

Emily and Sheba waited in the car while Aunt Risi and Mom went into the Real Estate Office. Emily had to laugh a little at Aunt Risi's outfit. Lederhosen, hiking boots, and her short dark hair tucked under a hat with a feather. "She is quite eccentric," she said to Sheba.

When Aunt Risi came back to the car, she said "We all must sleep with a window open tonight. It is the last night before the dark of the moon and we only want to hear good news about the mansion."

Yep, very eccentric, Emily thought, but she would sleep with her window open just to be sure.

Chapter II
Moving Day

"Aunt Risi's furniture is arriving today," Emily said. "I can't wait to get back to her house. She said Mimi would be here today and she had some cleaning done so that Mimi wouldn't try to do it."

"That's right," Mom said. "Your cousin Madison will also be here today with her Yellow Lab Max. I am happy she can come and spend some time with Aunt Risi and all of us."

"Oh, I didn't know Madison was coming," Emily said. "Aunt Risi said Zachary was coming."

"Zachary can't come, he's going to be a camp counselor for the next two weeks," Mom said. "It will be very good for him, and very good for you and Madison to get to know each other again. After all, it's been a year since they moved away.

"She was such a little kid when they moved. I can't imagine that she will be any different now," Emily said. "I don't really think it will be much fun to have her here, but it will be fun to meet Max, and Sheba will be happy to have another dog to play with."

"I hope someday they can all move back here. I miss having my family close."

"I know Mom, I miss them too."

"For now, we better get going. Aunt Risi is already at the house and Uncle Chris and Madison will be there later this morning. He's on his way to Oklahoma for business. I want to make sure I get a chance to see him before he has to leave."

On the drive to Aunt Risi's new home, Emily thought about Madison. When Madison and her family moved away, she was a very shy, very little girl and would barely talk to anyone. I know she can't be any different now. Having her here won't be any fun, but solving the mystery will be fun so I'll concentrate on that.

"It looks like the movers are already here," Emily said as they drove into Aunt Risi's driveway. "And look, Uncle Chris is standing out front."

They hurried and parked the car and Emily and Sheba ran to greet Uncle Chris, with mom close behind.

"It's so good to see you," Uncle Chris said, "Even if it is only for a few minutes. I will try to do better next time."

"I hope so," Mom said. "We want to see more of you and your whole family. I really miss you not being close by."

After Uncle Chris left, they went inside to see if they could help. Aunt Risi called them into the office, the only room that was not being invaded by the movers.

Madison, her gray hazel eyes shining, smiled as they came into the room. She and her Yellow Lab Max sat on the sofa with Aunt Risi. She jumped up to hug her Aunt Kathy and her cousin Emily.

"My you've grown," Aunt Kathy said. "And Max, aren't you handsome."

"Yes, you have grown," Emily said. "You were so little last year, and yes, Max you are very handsome.

Madison giggled, and said, "Sir Maximus, I would like you to meet the Queen of Sheba, and of course Aunt Kathy and Emily."

The dogs were already busy sniffing and bumping each other like long-lost family.

"It looks like they'll get along fine," Aunt Risi said. "I've been enjoying Madison's company and of course meeting Max. Madison has been telling me all the things she has done so far this summer. It all sounds so fun."

Well, Emily thought. She's grown lots taller and she's already talking more than she ever did when she was ten. Maybe this visit will be more interesting than I thought.

"We are kind of stuck in this room until the movers are done, so I thought it would be a good time to tell you what I have learned. The realtor was able to get the answers I wanted."

"The Pond family didn't actually move out of this house," she said. "They built the newer mansion because the family was growing so fast, they needed more room. The great-grandparents lived here their whole married life. The grandparents lived here until they got older, and the grandmother needed care. They moved to the newer house so the family could watch over her better. This house has been empty because they really didn't want anyone outside of the family to live here. They put it up for sale because the farm is suffering financially, and they really need the money."

"I hope it's enough to help them," Mom said.

"I don't know," Aunt Risi said. "I think it would cost a lot to operate a farm that size every month. Their income is from raising, training, and selling cutting horses. They have also always traveled the cutting horse circuit, showing their horses. They won a lot so they earned a very good living there, but they don't have anyone on the circuit right now. The realtor said the young son, Rob is training for the circuit, but he is only fourteen, so it will be a few years before he is ready, The Pond name is world famous in the cutting horse industry."

"Well, that explains a lot," Mom said. "Should we go check on the movers?"

"Yes," Aunt Risi said. "I want to make sure Mimi's room will be ready for her when she gets here. She'll be tired from traveling."

Emily and Madison smiled at each other as they watched Aunt Risi walk out in her brown Gaucho outfit.

"Very eccentric," Emily said.

"That's what Dad says," Madison told Emily. "Do you want to take the dogs outside?"

"Good idea," Emily said. "It's really nice out back. Maybe we could explore the barn while Mom and Aunt Risi finish up in the house."

"Maybe we can find a mystery like you and Zachary did," Madison said, her brown ponytail swinging as she walked.

"Maybe," Emily said. "But I kind of think we already have one. Are you sure you want to be involved?"

"Oh yes," Madison said, her gray hazel eyes shining. "It's what I hoped for ever since Dad and Mom said I could come here and stay with Aunt Risi and you. For once I'll have a great story to tell."

"Okay," Emily said. "Let's walk out to the barn and I will tell you what I have found."

"The first day we were here, when Aunt Risi was just looking at this house I found a very old police report in the desk drawer. It said that someone broke in here and stole several pieces of valuable jewelry and some gold coins. I didn't have time to search any further because Mom and Aunt Risi called me to go out back with them. I have a feeling that this crime has never been solved and I think the stolen items could very well be hidden around here somewhere. If we could find them, we could give them back to the family. It could be enough to help their financial problems."

"Where do we begin?" Madison asked as they followed the dogs inside the barn.

"Well, apparently not here," Emily said. "This place has been swept clean. All that's left are the empty horse stalls.

They walked around the barn and through each stall just in case whoever cleaned the barn missed something, but they didn't find anything.

"Let's go up in the loft. We may be able to see more of the area around us from up there. Sheba, stay down." Emily said as she started to climb the ladder to the loft.

Madison followed, giving Max the same command.

"The loft is as clean as the barn, Madison said. But the view is spectacular. Look, you can see a big pond or lake over there."

"Oh yes," Emily said. "That is way over behind the farm. I think we should explore over there, but we probably shouldn't trespass."

"Didn't Aunt Risi say there's a fourteen, year old boy at the farm?" Madison asked. "Maybe we could meet him, and we could all explore together."

"Very good thinking Madison," Emily said. "But first I think we should go back to the office to see if we can find some more information on the robbery. I don't think we should tell anyone about this yet. I would rather wait until we have something more than just the old police report.

"Okay," Madison agreed. "But we will have to tell the boy at the farm, won't we?"

"Not right away." Emily said. "We have to get to know him a little first, then we'll decide how much we should tell him."

The dogs waited while Emily and Madison came down from the loft.

"Let's walk out to the fence," Emily said. "The dogs deserve a bigger outing than just a trip to the barn. Besides, you never know where we might find some clues."